CHADWICK'S WEDDING

By
Priscilla Cummings

Illustrated by A.R.Cohen

Tidewater Publishers
Centreville, Maryland

Copyright © 1989 by Priscilla Cummings and A.R. Cohen
Manufactured in Hong Kong

Chadwick was confused. Living in a glass tank at the aquarium was fun, but it sure had its drawbacks. For one thing, there wasn't much privacy. And now that he and Esmerelda were thinking of getting married and having a family, Chadwick worried whether there would be enough room. Toddler crabs, after all, need lots of space to swim and play games.

On the other hand, an aquarium was an educational place to raise children. Chadwick had met so many different fish and animals at the aquarium, he felt like a world traveler even though he had never left Baltimore and the Chesapeake Bay.

One night, he started thinking about his big decision, and he couldn't sleep. He went upstairs, tiptoed past the poison frogs and skittered into the rain forest. There he spied his friend, Charlie, the two-toed sloth.

Chadwick waited as Charlie sluggishly made his way down a fig tree, hung upside down from the lowest branch, and stared at the fruits and vegetables in his food pan.

"What's wrong?" Chadwick asked. "You sick?"

Slowly, the sloth looked down at Chadwick. Everything Charlie did, he did slowly. "Nooooo," he said.

There was a pause, and Chadwick sighed, knowing he'd have to wait awhile for the rest of the answer.

"I'm . . . just bored . . . that's all."

"Gee," Chadwick replied, "how could you be bored with all these interesting trees to climb?"

Minutes seemed to pass. The sloth shifted position. "Chadwick . . . ," he began, taking a long, deep breath, "how would you . . . like to spend your life . . . upside down?"

Chadwick flipped over on his shell and gazed up through the thick, green foliage toward the glass roof above. Stars dotted the velvet night like bright sequins, and moonlight fell softly through the exotic ferns and palms. The splashing of several waterfalls made a soothing sound. For a moment, Chadwick imagined he was lying on the warm sand of a remote, tropical island. "I don't know—it's pretty nice."

Charlie scoffed, "Don't be silly . . . it's a rightside-up world . . . and, Chadwick . . . , it's passing me by."

The crab rolled back onto his legs and nodded with understanding. There was a time when he, too, felt restless. "What you need is a rightside-up adventure!" Chadwick suggested. "Stand up on your hind legs and go see the world!"

Charlie's drowsy brown eyes opened wide. "Gosh, that would be great!" he exclaimed. But then he slumped again. His eyelids drooped and his mouth pinched together in a pout. He reached for a chunk of sweet potato and toyed with the food. "Forget it," he said sadly. "I don't have . . . anywhere to go."

Chadwick hated to see a friend feel so low. Crossing his pinchers, he frowned, deep in thought. "Say, Charlie! Why don't you come to my wedding at Shady Creek? You could hop a barge and take your time coming down." Chadwick chuckled to himself. Of course Charlie would take his time—he always took his time!

The sloth let go of the branch and landed on the ground beside Chadwick. Thump! His eyes sparkled with excitement. "You're getting married? This is big news!"

Chadwick smiled. "But we still haven't decided where to live and raise our children," he said. "Anyway, what do you say? Will you come to the wedding?"

Charlie's round face broke into a wide grin. "Chadwick, I wouldn't miss it for the world!"

Just then, a nosy, yellow parrot with bright green wings flew down and butted into their conversation. "Wedding? Wedding? Who's having a wedding?" she cackled.

Chadwick rolled his eyes and sighed: "I am, Penelope."

"Well, well! How charming! Weddings are my specialty. I organize them from start to finish."

"Penelope, everything's arranged."

The parrot's beak was still half open. "But I write a great invitation."

"They're done," Chadwick insisted, "here, look." He pulled two envelopes from under his shell.

With a haughty sniff, Penelope ripped hers open and read:

Chadwick and Esmerelda
invite you to their wedding.
To be held at low tide,
during the full moon
of October,
at the Shady Creek Sandbar.
Reception following.

"Well, you'll need someone to conduct the ceremony," she squawked. "I could do that."

Chadwick looked doubtful. "Baron von Heron is writing something special. You don't know him, Penelope, but he's a great blue heron who has a special way with words."

"Hmmmmph," Penelope grunted, "then I'll sing at the reception. I have a terrific voice. B-r-o-c-k-k-k-k-k-!"

Charlie wrapped his long arms over his head to cover his ears, and Chadwick winced. "Thanks, Penelope!" the crab shouted. "But my Uncle Fred is coming up from North Carolina with the Fiddler Crab Band."

Penelope stopped singing. "Flowers," she said, "I could arrange the flowers."

"My friend, Matilda the egret, is taking care of that."

"The cake then . . . ," Penelope suggested hopefully.

Chadwick sighed. "Toulouse, a French Canada goose I know, has been working on the recipe for weeks. He's a gourmet goose, you see. He's making something special with corn and eelgrass."

"Oh, yuck," Penelope said, turning her head.

Chadwick began to feel sorry for her. "Listen," he said, "would you like to take care of the guest book, Penelope?"

"Sure!" she agreed happily.

Relieved, Chadwick bid a quick farewell. He'd already been out of the water too long and his shell was starting to itch.

Charlie grabbed the branch with his strong claws and hung upside down again to eat. Just thinking about his upcoming adventure had given him a big appetite.

As he stuffed another lettuce leaf into his mouth, Charlie stared at the top right corner of the rain forest and caught sight of Rapunzel lazily inching downward through the bamboo. She was such a lovely sloth with her long, carefully groomed hair and her cute, pug nose. When she hung upside down, her slender arms and legs gracefully embraced the tree branches.

Charlie had been brought all the way from a zoo in Salisbury, Maryland, to keep Rapunzel company, a match that would have overjoyed any other sloth. But the fact of the matter was, Charlie simply didn't love her. At least he didn't think so.

He stopped eating. "Gosh," he murmured, "what is love anyway? And how will I know when it's real?"

Funny, but as Chadwick made his way back to his tank, he was wondering the same thing.

*   *   *

All the way back to Shady Creek, Esmerelda chatted excitedly about the wedding plans.

"I finally decided on my bridesmaids," she said.

"I'm going to ask Christina Claws and Betty Blue. Shell-ey, of course, will be my maid of honor."

Chadwick was only half listening.

"What about you?" Esmerelda went on. "Have you decided on a best man?"

Chadwick continued to swim.

"Chadwick?" Esmerelda had to grab one of his swimming legs to slow him down. "What are you thinking about? You look worried."

"Oh . . . nothing. I'm sorry. What did you ask me?"

A nervous feeling swept over Esmerelda. She wondered if Chadwick was having second thoughts about getting married.

"I said," she gulped and tried to sound cheerful, "have you decided on a best man?"

"Yes. As a matter of fact, I have," Chadwick replied. "I've asked Bernie the Sea Gull. He's my best friend, after all."

Esmerelda moaned. "Your grandmother will have a fit."

"I know," Chadwick said. His grandmother disapproved of Bernie. She thought he was a selfish, loud-mouthed gull whose only concern was his next meal. Chadwick could never convince her that Bernie had a kind and generous side to him as well.

But this was not the only thing on Chadwick's mind. Although Toulouse said he would arrive from Canada before the full moon of October, Chadwick knew a strong head wind from the southeast could delay the flock for days.

And, as Esmerelda had feared, Chadwick had yet another worry: He still wasn't sure that getting married was the right thing to do. After all, this was a decision he would have to live with for the rest of his life!

As he swam on, Chadwick tried to put his worries aside. A couple times, he and Esmerelda surfaced so they could enjoy the colorful autumn leaves that shaded their favorite coves. The first days of fall used to make Chadwick sad because they meant winter was coming. But ever since he had moved into the aquarium, he didn't have to spend the long, cold months trying to sleep at the bottom of the bay.

After a full day of swimming, Chadwick and Esmerelda
rounded the sandbar at Shady Creek, happy, but hungry
and tired. All they wanted was a good meal and some soft
mud in which to rest. Their friends had other ideas.
Esmerelda's girlfriends swept her off to a far corner of
the marsh to talk about the wedding plans. Chadwick
was surrounded by his own noisy gang.

"Hey! Welcome home!" Bug-Eyed Benny called
out.

Bernie splashed down and floated over to the crabs.
"Good to see you, Chadwick!"

"Yeah, congratulations!" Pincher Pete said, slapping
Chadwick on his shell. "So you're gonna get hitched, huh?"

Chadwick shrugged, "I guess so . . . "

"Well, don't worry, Chad," Pincher Pete said with
a mischievous gleam in his eye, "we're gonna give you
a stag party you won't forget!"

"A what?" Chadwick looked at Bernie.

"A stag party," Bernie repeated, "you know, to
say good-bye to being single."

Pincher Pete winked and nudged Chadwick with the joint of one claw. "We've already rented the Sunken Skiff Saloon."

Oh, dear, Chadwick thought to himself. Everyone in Shady Creek knew how noisy parties got at the Sunken Skiff Saloon. Sometimes, when the parties didn't stop, the Bluefish Patrol had to arrest everyone!

Chadwick moaned; one thing he *didn't* need was to spend the night before his wedding in the fishnet jail!

Just then, Hector Spector the Jellyfish blobbed by. "Oh, me, oh, my," he whined. "I was going to get you a basket of fish scraps for a wedding gift. Now I can't make up my mind. A set of clam shell dinner plates would make a better gift, right?"

Chadwick insisted there was nothing he needed. "Just come and enjoy the wedding," he told Hector Spector.

Turning back to the sea gull, Chadwick said, "Listen, Bernie, I really need to talk to you about something important."

Bernie shook his head. "Not now, Chadwick. I've got to find a tuxedo that fits. I guess it's all this junk food I've been eating . . . " He glanced down at his big belly and frowned. "It's probably too late to diet now."

Come to think of it, Bernie had put on a few ounces, Chadwick noticed.

Bernie rearranged his wing feathers. "Oh . . . by the way, I promised Orville I'd give you this note."

"Wait, I need to talk to you!" Chadwick called out. "I'm having doubts about . . . " But Bernie flew off, muttering to himself about cutting down on French fries and cookie crumbs.

Wearily, Chadwick opened the note and read aloud:

Dear Chadwick,

I'm sorry, but I can't attend your wedding on the sandbar. We oysters never leave our beds. I hope you understand. Thanks anyway and best wishes.

Orville the Oyster

Hector Spector groaned. "Oh, great. I suppose Orville and his rich Uncle Rockefeller will send the most expensive gift. No, maybe not. Dr. Mallard's pretty rich, too . . . "

Chadwick was trying to think of how Orville could get a lift to the wedding when Grandmother Crab, who had come all the way from Solomons Island, approached with her claws on her hips and her eyestalks raised angrily.

"What's the meaning of this, young crab?" she demanded. "My only grandchild gets married, and he asks a sea gull to be his best man? Your mother and father, bless their souls, would not have allowed it! A crab should have crabs in his wedding! What about your good friends, Pincher Pete and Bug-Eyed Benny?"

"They're ushers, Grandma. They'll be in the wedding, too."

Chadwick's grandmother was not satisfied. "What about Chicken Necker Ned or Brickle Bottom Bob then?"

"But Grandma, Bernie is my best friend! What does it matter that he has feathers instead of a shell? Or that he has two legs instead of ten? He has a good heart, and he's been my buddy since the first day I swam into Shady Creek!"

There was no letup for the next two days. It was just one problem after another.

Matilda kept warning Chadwick that the wedding must run on time. "I'm not going to pick flowers and watch them wilt," she grumbled.

Pincher Pete kept making jokes about the stag party. Toulouse still hadn't arrived. Uncle Fred and the Fiddler Crab Band were delayed by strong ocean currents. Hector Spector bent himself all out of shape with worry about getting the right gift. And Bernie kept popping the studs on every tuxedo he tried on!

Then, to top it all off,
Baron von Heron complained
that he couldn't write the
wedding ceremony. He kept
loosening his ascot and saying:

"Oh, Chadwick—it is awfully tough
to write a wedding good enough
for Esmerelda and for you.
Oh, goodness me!
What will I do?"

Chadwick was about to throw up his claws and scream when Shell-ey swam up to him with tears streaming down her face.

"It's Esmerelda!" she sobbed. "We've looked all over for her, Chadwick, but she's disappeared!"

*   *   *

Meanwhile, on a barge on the bay, in the sun of midday, a sloth hung upside down beneath a pile of packing crates and grinned ear-to-ear. Staring at the blue water above and the blue sky below, Charlie was the happiest he'd been in years.

Occasionally, he glanced at a map Chadwick had given him. "Be careful," the crab had instructed, "forty-some different rivers empty into the bay. You don't want to jump off at the wrong place."

Charlie decided he liked traveling so much that, after the wedding, he would continue his cruise down the Chesapeake to see the islands—Smith and Tangier, that is. In his wildest daydreams, he even imagined hopping a freighter to visit his relatives in Central America.

Penelope perched beside Charlie and jabbered away. But Charlie didn't mind the parrot's endless chatter. He closed his eyes and enjoyed the warm breeze, which blew through his long, coarse hair like an invisible comb.

"I can see why Chadwick loves the bay so much. Personally, however, it's not humid enough out here for me," he said to Penelope in surprisingly quick, smooth sentences. Now that Charlie had so many exciting plans, he didn't want to waste time talking so slowly.

Penelope smiled. She was enjoying her Chesapeake adventure, too. Little did she and Charlie know that everything was going haywire at Shady Creek.

*   *   *

After looking for Esmerelda in all her favorite places, Chadwick began to panic: What if she'd been kidnapped? Or worse, caught in a crab pot somewhere?

Uncle Fred and the other fiddlers arrived, only to put down their music and join the hunt. Chadwick's grandmother summoned Bernie to help. And Bernie, in turn, got all the gulls to conduct an air search.

Belly Jeans the Flounder recruited his fish buddies to scour the bay floor. Even the Bluefish Patrol was put on alert and issued a bulletin:

> MISSING: SHE-CRAB. ON SMALL SIDE. CURLY
> EYELASHES. LAST SEEN WEARING A BRACELET
> ON RIGHT CLAW. ANSWERS TO ESMERELDA.

Matilda tried to assist, but the excitement was too much for her and she fainted—right on the bed of goldenrod she'd been eyeing for the wedding bouquet.

"Esmerelda! Esmerelda! Where are you, sweetheart?" Chadwick called out at the top of his gills. When there was no answer, he swam on, checking between rocks and calling out again and again.

Every once in a while, he surfaced and scanned the water for sight of any long, narrow workboats and the men who might be hauling in their crab pots. But while he didn't see any workboats, he did see Bernie and signaled with his claws.

"Any luck?" he hollered as the sea gull splashed down.

"Nothing," Bernie said. "You don't think she's run off, do you?"

Chadwick froze. It hadn't occurred to him that Esmerelda might have run off. Golly, he thought, maybe she had second thoughts about the wedding, too, and had decided she couldn't go through with it!

Dismayed, Chadwick sank up to his eyes. His legs hung limp in the water. "My life is a complete shambles," he mumbled sadly. "Without Esmerelda, I can't go on."

"Hey, now," Bernie said, "don't jump to conclusions. Why, everybody knows you two love each other!"

Chadwick nodded. He now knew for certain that he loved Esmerelda with all his heart. And there was no doubt that he wanted to marry her.

"See you later—I've got to keep on looking," Chadwick said before disappearing beneath the surface.

The search continued all night and all the next day until evening approached. Then, one by one, the crabs crawled back to Shady Creek. Even the gulls gave up and had to rest their weary wings.

Bernie was the only one who continued to crisscross the water. As the sun set, turning the sky into a sea of orange and red, he perched on a dock piling and peered through his binoculars. Rocks . . . a broken oar . . . even an abandoned canoe came into focus. Suddenly—what was this? A small claw waving weakly in the marsh grass?

Bernie took off and swooped lower for a better look.
"Are you all right?" he asked as he landed quickly on
a thin strip of beach. Esmerelda lay on her back in a
shallow pool of water, all tangled up in a plastic six-pack
holder.

"I'm so glad to see you, Bernie. I came out here to
be by myself and think about things when I got stuck in
this trash."

"Well, you're lucky," Bernie consoled her. "At least
you're alive. A bird I knew choked to death on one of
these things. Now hold on, I'll get you out."

Bernie bit down on the plastic rings and tugged
on them, dragging Esmerelda in the sand. On the second
tug, however, the rings slipped off so easily that Bernie
tumbled backwards into the creek!

Esmerelda giggled. "Thanks," she said as Bernie shook the water from his wings.

"My pleasure," he replied.

Back at the Shady Creek Sandbar, Bernie was greeted as a hero—especially by Chadwick's grandmother, who had never thought much of sea gulls before.

"Esmerelda!" Chadwick exclaimed, relieved and happy to see her. "Where were you? What happened?"

She looked down at her pinchers and dragged a dainty claw in the mud. Chadwick loved it when she did that. "It doesn't matter what happened," she said, "what's important is that I decided we shouldn't be married if you have doubts. I love you and I don't want you to be unhappy."

Chadwick picked up her claw, brushed the mud off, and squeezed it. "The only thing that would make me *unhappy,* Esmerelda, is if you *didn't* marry me."

Loud, noisy shouting burst forth from behind them, for everyone had been shamelessly eavesdropping. "HOORAY," the crowd yelled, "THE WEDDING'S ON!"

* * *

As the tide retreated and the moon rose, Uncle Fred and the other fiddlers warmed up, their music carrying far and wide in the thin night air. Crickets chirped to the beat, and a pair of swans in a nearby inlet stretched their necks and trumpeted a magnificent chorus.

Matilda was too busy to enjoy the music. Fussing and fuming, she arranged a splendid bouquet of goldenrod and cattails, then decorated the sandbar with seaweed streamers.

Toulouse, honking to announce his arrival, waddled in with a gigantic cornmeal cake laced with gooey, green eelgrass frosting. "It eeze spectacular, no?" he asked everyone.

And Bernie finally had a tuxedo that fit—thanks to Chadwick's grandmother, who let out the seams and sewed them back up with fishing line that wouldn't break. Proudly, Bernie strutted down the sandbar as he showed Dr. and Mrs. Mallard to their seats.

Belly Jeans floundered nearby, passing the time with members of the Bluefish Patrol, who had tucked their hats under their fins. After the reception, the patrol planned to escort Chadwick and Esmerelda to their honeymoon cove in the Wye River.

"Out of my way, fish!" Matilda grumped as she stepped through the water to fix a Black-eyed Susan on each of the boy crabs' shells. Squinting, she admired her work, then handed the bride a tiny spray of Queen Anne's lace. "It's time we got started," she whispered to the nervous group.

But Chadwick wasn't quite ready. "Just another minute," he begged. "I know Charlie and Penelope will be here soon."

Sure enough, just seconds later, a small rowboat rounded the bend. Everyone laughed at the sight of a sloth pulling on the oars and a parrot perched on the bow!

As soon as the boat was beached on the sand, Chadwick turned and nodded to Baron von Heron.

His Birdship took his cue and cleared his throat with confidence, for words had come back to him in great abundance.

"Now hush, my friends! It's been agreed.
 The sandbar wedding must proceed!"

At the Baron's urging, the large crowd fell silent. Birds

sat, fish froze in place, eels wriggled into the back row,
and crabs scuttled to the front. Turtles lumbered onto the
sandbar, and the otters made one, last playful splash
before settling down.

There were so many friends in attendance that
there was barely room for Chadwick and Esmerelda
to inch sideways, single file, down the aisle. Finally,
they made their way to stand, claw in claw, before Baron
von Heron, who lifted his head and continued:

> "If love is true when two crabs wed
> it will endure—or so it's said.
> But just remember, if you will,
> the bay's not always calm and still.
> When dark clouds cover up the sky,
> when creeks are rough and waves are high,
> then swim together, side by side,
> and you will easily ride the tide."

27

The Baron paused a moment and waited for Chadwick and Esmerelda to nod their understanding. When they did, he adjusted his monocle and finished up:

"Bay bless you both. Good luck in life!
I now pronounce you Crab and Wife!"

Chadwick and Esmerelda squeezed pinchers and kissed quickly for they were both very shy. Baron von Heron smiled broadly and turned to the guests:

"Now, Fred! Please fiddle up a tune!
Let's celebrate beneath the moon!"

"Congratulations!" their friends yelled, tossing fluffy milkweed seeds into the air and swarming around the newlyweds for hugs and clawshakes.

Pincher Pete rang the wedding shells while Toulouse carved up the cake. "Delicious," Bernie commented, stuffing another piece into his beak.

Penelope busied herself getting everyone to sign the guest book, but couldn't convince Hector Spector, who was undecided whether he should sign, "Hector Spector the Jellyfish" or "Hector Spector the Sea Nettle."

"A toast to your marriage," said Charlie, as he lifted a nutshell of blackberry juice. "And, by the way, I want to say good-bye."

"Good-bye?"

"Yes. I understand you and Esmerelda have decided to live in the bay until the children are raised."

"It's home, after all," Chadwick explained. "When the children are grown, they can decide whether they want to live in the aquarium with us. But we'll see you again then."

"I'm afraid not," Charlie said, "I won't be in Baltimore."

"What?" Chadwick asked, not sure he heard right.

"I found out what love is," Charlie said with a knowing grin. "Yes. It's when you realize you can't live without that special someone—or something."

Chadwick nodded for he knew that was true.

"Seeing new places, making new friends. That's my passion in life," Charlie went on. "I'm going to ask for a transfer immediately. I hope to go overseas—the Far East, maybe."

"What about Rapunzel?" Chadwick asked.

"She'll be better off," Charlie replied. "She deserves a more settled and slower-moving sloth than me."

Chadwick was surprised, but he understood. After all, he still believed that if you have a dream, you should go after it.

Just then, Uncle Fred introduced a fat bullfrog named Harry, who croaked out the square dance calls in his deep voice:

"All right, my friends, let's circle round.
We'll dance all night to the fiddler's sound!
Come choose your partner, swing her high;
Then turn and smile and wink your eye!"

Chadwick put his claw around Esmerelda, sure that their dream of a happy life together now would come true.

"Look," Esmerelda said, chuckling, "Bernie's dancing with your grandmother!"

Laughing, they joined the circle as the joyous sounds of their wedding filled every corner of Shady Creek and echoed long into the moonlit night.